REP   NOV 1998

D0149773

The Mystery of the Hobo's Message

THREE COUSINS DETECTIVE CLUB®

———————

9610

The Mystery of the Hobo's Message

Elspeth Campbell Murphy
Illustrated by Joe Nordstrom

BETHANY HOUSE PUBLISHERS
MINNEAPOLIS, MINNESOTA 55438

NORTH CENTRAL REGIONAL LIBRARY
Headquarters Wenatchee WA

Cover and story illustrations by Joe Nordstrom

Three Cousins Detective Club® and TCDC® are registered trademarks of Elspeth Campbell Murphy

Copyright © 1995
Elspeth Campbell Murphy

All rights reserved. No part of this publication may be reproduced, stored in a retrieval system, or transmitted in any form or by any means electronic, mechanical, photocopying, recording, or otherwise without the prior written permission of the publisher and copyright owners.

Published by Bethany House Publishers
A Ministry of Bethany Fellowship, Inc.
11300 Hampshire Avenue South
Minneapolis, Minnesota 55438

Printed in the United States of America.

Library of Congress Cataloging-in-Publication Data

Murphy, Elspeth Campbell.
    The mystery of the hobo's message / Elspeth Campbell Murphy.
       p.   cm. — (Three Cousins Detective Club® ; bk.5)
    Summary: When the three cousins find some strange symbols carved in an old tree, they start learning about hobo code and in the process learn about the importance of kindness as well.

    [1. Mystery and detective stories. 2. Tramps—Fiction.
3. Cousins—Fiction. 4. Twins—Fiction. 5. Christian life—Fiction.]
I. Title. II. Series: Murphy, Elspeth Campbell. Three Cousins Detective Club™ ; 5.
PZ7.M95316Mych   1995
[Fic]—dc20   94–49224
ISBN 1–55661–409–8   CIP
                                      AC

NORTH CENTRAL REGIONAL LIBRARY
Headquarters Wenatchee, WA

In loving memory of my father-in-law,
Howard R. Murphy,
whose life was filled with
love, joy, peace,
patience, kindness, goodness,
faithfulness, gentleness, and self-control.

1

Cat Man

*M*uch as he loved animals, Titus McKay was not too crazy about cats. That was probably why cats were so crazy about him. Titus had noticed something about cats. They always seemed to go to the people who didn't particularly want them.

At least that was true of his grandparents' two cats. Whenever Titus and his cousins sat down to work on their code books or something, the cats came running. They loved to drape themselves across Titus's shoulders. Titus kept peeling them off. But they always came back.

Titus's cousin, Timothy Dawson, thought this was hilarious. He called Titus "Cat Man."

Titus's other cousin, Sarah-Jane Cooper,

thought it was unfair. No matter how much she pleaded, "Here, kitty, kitty," the cats climbed all over Titus.

Titus's Yorkshire terrier, Gubbio, thought it was outrageous. Titus was *his* boy, after all. At first, Gubbio had tried to chase the cats away. But they had just looked at him as if they were looking at air. If he barked at them, they just meowed sweetly as if to say, "Dog? What dog? We don't see a dog."

Finally, Gubbio gave up trying to get rid of the cats. But whenever they jumped on Titus's shoulders, he jumped on Titus's lap.

Titus was the first to admit that nothing made a house look more homey than pets— even cats. But having them around made it hard to get stuff done. Granted, Titus and his cousins were on vacation at their grandparents' house. But they still wanted to get stuff done. Their code books, for example.

The cousins had a detective club. And they wanted to be able to pass secret messages to one another.

They were working on this—or trying to— when their grandfather came by. He was a pastor, and he was on his way to his study in the church next door.

He said with a straight face, "Rather hot to be wearing a fur coat, isn't it, Titus?"

11

"Grandpa, will you please take them with you?" Titus pleaded.

Grandpa laughed. *Sometimes* the cats would come when he called.

But before he could try it, the phone rang.

Grandpa sighed. "I hope it's not those developers again," he said. "They've been calling every day and sometimes twice a day. I don't know what I'm going to do."

The cousins looked at one another in surprise. It was not often that their grandfather didn't know what to do. What was going on?

2

The Sweetest House

*T*he cousins knew it was impolite to listen in on other people's conversations. But their grandfather *had* taken the call in the kitchen. And he *hadn't* asked them to leave. Besides, there might be some way they could help. You never could tell.

"No, I haven't reached a decision yet," said Grandpa, sounding weary but firm. "No, the house isn't listed with a real estate agent. . . . Yes, it will be a private sale. . . . No, I'm not at liberty to quote you a price. . . . Yes, the terms were very specific. . . . No, I can't tell you what they were. That's confidential. . . . Yes, I will let you know when I've made up my mind. . . . No, there's really no need for you to call again tomorrow. . . . Yes, I will let you know. . . .

Yes. . . . Yes, I will. . . . No, that won't be necessary. . . . Yes. . . . Goodbye."

"Arrrghh!" said Grandpa when he had hung up the phone. "They say the squeaky wheel gets the grease. But these people really are impossible!"

"Grandpa!" cried Sarah-Jane, looking wide-eyed with alarm. "You're not selling the house, are you?"

"Oh, no, sweetheart," Grandpa assured her. "I'm not selling *our* house. I'm selling *a* house."

"Huh?" said Timothy.

"Come again?" said Titus.

"It's a cottage, really," explained Grandpa. "And it belonged to old Mrs. Willowby. You remember Mrs. Willowby, don't you? She was a member of the church for longer than anyone."

The cousins nodded. Just thinking of old Mrs. Willowby made them smile. She had always been so kind to them. To everyone. But thinking about her made them feel sad, too, because they knew she had died not that long ago.

"Anyway," said Grandpa. "Mrs. Willowby had no family. She asked me to find just the right people and sell them her cottage. It's all in her will, and I have to honor her wishes. But her house sits on a lovely piece of property. A lot of people would love to get their hands on it."

"Is there anything we can do to help?" asked Titus. He didn't really think there was. It didn't sound like the kind of thing a kid could do.

Grandpa smiled. "Thanks for the offer. I'll keep it in mind. Right now, you can help by keeping me company. I want to ride over and check on the cottage."

When most grown-ups said "ride," they meant in a car. When Grandpa said "ride," he meant on his bicycle.

The cousins had brought their bikes with them. And soon all four of them were pedaling along through the little resort town where Pastor and Mrs. Gordon lived.

The cousins had never seen Mrs. Willowby's cottage. They stopped their bikes and looked down on it from a little hill.

Titus said the first thing that popped into his head. "The cottage looks like her."

Everybody laughed. But it was the kind of laugh you give when someone says something odd that you know is absolutely true.

Titus was right. The house *did* look like Mrs. Willowby. Small and trim and peaceful. As if having a person like Mrs. Willowby live inside it all those years had somehow rubbed off on the house itself.

"It's just the *sweetest* house!" declared Sarah-Jane. And although they might not have put it that way, the men had to agree.

It was only when they got closer that they noticed the two kids sitting on the porch. A boy and a girl, who looked to be the same age

16

as the cousins. And who looked almost exactly like each other. Twins?

They were staring anxiously up into a tree.

3

A Job for Cat Man

"What seems to be the trouble here?" Grandpa asked them kindly.

The boy and girl jumped. Apparently they had been so intent on the tree that they hadn't heard Grandpa and the cousins ride up.

For a moment the two kids just stared at them in alarm. In fact, Titus thought they were about to run away. But they didn't seem to want to leave the tree.

"It's our cat," said the girl at last. "He climbed up there. And now he can't get down."

They all peered up into the branches at the pretty little orange-striped cat. He was bigger than a kitten, but not quite full-grown. He meowed piteously down at them.

Titus stood back, rubbed his chin, and studied the situation. He had seen this type of thing before.

"What's his name?" Sarah-Jane asked the girl.

"He doesn't have one yet," she replied. "We just got him yesterday."

"Actually, he's not exactly ours," the boy corrected. "He's a stray that just sort of adopted us."

"That means *he* thinks he's ours," persisted the girl. "Or that we're his. And either way, we can't just leave him up there." She sounded on the verge of tears.

"Here, kitty, kitty," said Sarah-Jane, wanting to help. But her track record of getting cats to come to her was not very good. And even she didn't sound very hopeful.

Timothy stepped forward and said boldly, "Obviously, somebody has to go up there and bring the cat down." He paused. "I nominate Cat Man."

"I second the motion!" cried Sarah-Jane joyously.

Grandpa said, "It has been moved and seconded that Titus Gordon McKay—otherwise known as Cat Man—be given the task of getting the cat in question down from said tree. All in favor, say 'aye.' "

"Aye!" yelled everyone, including the boy and girl, who laughed in spite of themselves.

Titus nodded. He had expected as much. In fact, he had already worked out in his head the best way up.

Cat Man was a good nickname for him not just because cats adored him. It was also a good nickname because he could climb as well as any cat. Better. At least *he* knew how to get down. He had rescued a few cats in his day, and he had even worked out a system.

His method was to climb up slowly and casually. He would get as close to the cat as possible. And completely ignore it. It never failed. All he had to do was wait, and the cat would come to him. Once the cat was holding on to him, Titus could climb down for both of them.

Grandpa gave him a boost, and Titus swung himself onto the lowest branch. From there he began to climb according to the route he had mapped out down below.

He got to the branch he was aiming for.

Then he settled down to wait without so much as a glance at the cat.

It was nice up there, Titus thought. The sunlight played tag with the leaves, and little bugs ran up and down the trunk.

But suddenly Titus noticed something. Something very, very odd.

4

Tree Pictures

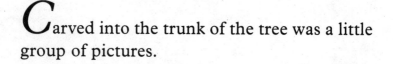

*C*arved into the trunk of the tree was a little group of pictures.

There was a top hat:

A smiling cat:

A kind of tent:

And a little circle inside a circle:

What in the world? Titus had seen initials carved on a tree, but never anything like this. So he held on to the branch with one hand and dug into his pocket with the other. He pulled out the little notebook and pencil stub he always carried. Balancing carefully, he copied the pictures exactly as they appeared on the tree.

The pictures weren't hard to copy. They were just simple little drawings. But Titus didn't think they were just meaningless doodles, either. He didn't know *what* they were.

He was so busy thinking about the pictures that he forgot all about the cat. He didn't have to pretend to ignore it. It just worked out that way.

But the cat couldn't ignore Titus.

It landed with a little "thwup!" on his shoulder. Titus almost fell off his branch in surprise.

He shoved the notebook and pencil stub in his pocket and started carefully down. He didn't want to startle the cat with any sudden noise or movement. So he acted like: Cat? What cat? I don't see a cat.

By the time they were safely down, the cat was sick and tired of being ignored. So when Sarah-Jane and the other girl rushed over, calling it a poor, sweet baby, the cat just ate it up. And to Sarah-Jane's great delight, the cat let her cuddle him.

"Oh, were you scared way up there in that great big tree?" she cooed.

"No," said Titus. "But thanks for asking."

The others, who had gotten acquainted while Titus was up in the tree, all laughed and burst into applause while Titus took a bow.

Titus found out that his first guess was right. The boy and girl were twins. He learned their names were Matthew and Amanda Jennings and that they were just visiting.

Sarah-Jane and Amanda were still fussing over the cat. And that reminded Titus of the smiling cat and the other drawings on the tree. He pulled out his notebook.

None of the kids knew what to make of them, either. But Grandpa looked long and hard at the drawings.

"Well, I'll be!" he said softly, more to himself than to anyone else. "I haven't seen the likes of these in more than fifty years."

5

The Hobo Code

*T*he kids all stared at him.

Timothy said, "You mean you've seen pictures like these before? In some other place?"

"Oh, yes," said Grandpa with a faraway look in his eyes. "What we have here is a hobo code."

The cousins looked a question at one another. They knew what a code was. And they sort of knew what a hobo was. But what was a hobo code?

Grandpa sat down on the porch. And from the way he settled in, the cousins knew he was about to Explain Something. Timothy, Titus, and Sarah-Jane settled in around him. And— with an uncertain glance at each other— Matthew and Amanda sat down, too. Their cat, of course, sat on Titus.

"Now," said Grandpa. "The first thing you have to understand about a hobo is that he didn't want to be called a tramp or a bum. Tramps and bums were not honest people, and they didn't want to work. A hobo, on the other hand, thought of himself as an honest, wandering worker. Some hoboes wandered because there was no work back home. Other hoboes wandered because they liked the adventure of moving from place to place."

"Sounds like it could be kind of fun, I guess," said Titus.

"That's what my father thought," said Grandpa with a twinkle in his eye.

The cousins stared at him. "You mean our great-grandfather was a *hobo*?" Sarah-Jane squeaked. It sounded kind of unreal.

Grandpa laughed. "For a while, yes. When he was a teenager. This was long before I was born."

"Did he carry his stuff in a bandanna on a stick?" asked Timothy.

"It was called a bindle," said Grandpa. "Like bundle. And a worker was called a stiff.

So another name for a wandering worker was a 'bindle stiff.' "

Titus loved the sound of that. He said thoughtfully, "Our great-grandfather was a bindle stiff. . . . But, Grandpa, what do the little pictures have to do with hoboes?"

"Well," said Grandpa. "The life of a hobo might have been fun in some ways. But it could be pretty lonely. And it could also be very dangerous. You never knew what to expect when you came to a new place.

"So the hoboes figured out a way to help one another—a secret code of pictures. When a hobo passed through a place, he would kindly leave a message for the hoboes who would come after him. The message was in the form of a little picture that told them what to expect. My father taught the code to me."

Titus pointed to his notebook. "So what do these pictures mean?"

6

The Willowbys

*E*veryone crowded around eagerly.

"Well, let's see if I can remember," said Grandpa. "The top hat stood for a gentleman. The Willowbys lived in this house for about as long as anyone can remember. So this hat must have stood for Mr. Willowby. And if anyone could be called a gentleman, it was Mr. Willowby. What a kind and generous person he was!

"Now, the smiling cat—that stood for a kindhearted woman."

"Mrs. Willowby!" cried Sarah-Jane.

"It would certainly fit her, wouldn't it?" said Grandpa. "If a hungry hobo, down on his luck, saw a drawing like this little smiling cat, he knew a kindhearted woman lived there.

And she would give him something to eat.

"The next picture of a little tentlike thing meant it was a good jungle, and you could make yourself at home."

"A jungle?" asked Timothy.

"Another word for a hobo camp," said Grandpa. "The Willowbys must have let the hoboes camp on their land. Not everyone would have done that.

"And, if I remember correctly, the little circle inside the bigger circle meant 'very good.' "

Grandpa was quiet for a moment. Then he said thoughtfully. "You know, I never knew this about the Willowbys—that they gave a helping hand to the hoboes. But given Mrs. Willowby's concern for the homeless, it certainly fits."

Matthew and Amanda shifted restlessly. And then they all seemed to realize that they had been sitting in one position too long.

As Titus stretched, he looked up at the tree. "Why put the code up so high?" he asked. "Who in the world would see it up there?"

"It wasn't up that high when it was carved," said Grandpa. "Remember, the days of the hoboes died out with the passing of the railroad. There are still trains, of course, but not as many as there once were. And hoboes depended on the freight trains for hitching rides."

Titus thought about that for a minute. "Oh, I see what you're saying! Hobo days were a long time ago, right? So the tree grew. And the pictures got carried up high."

"Exactly right," said Grandpa.

Timothy said, "So probably no one has even seen those pictures in years and years. Not until Titus came along."

"And Hobo," said Amanda.

She and Matthew had been listening so quietly that now it was almost as if the tree had said something.

"Who's Hobo?" asked Sarah-Jane. "Oh, the *cat*! Right? *Cute name!*"

"Wait a minute," said Matthew to his sister. "Don't I get a vote on what to call him?"

"Nope," said Amanda. "He likes the name Hobo."

Matthew shrugged. He seemed to know when it was useless to argue. "OK. Hobo it is. It *is* a good name, I guess. Well, we'd better get going."

He picked up Hobo, who had climbed on Titus's head and was trying to knock his glasses off. "Thanks for getting our cat, Titus!"

Titus gladly handed Hobo over. "That's OK. No problem."

"See you around," said Matthew.

"Yes, see you," said Amanda a little wistfully.

The twins got on their bikes and rode off. They were already well down the road when the cousins remembered something they wanted to ask them.

"Wait a minute," called Timothy. "Where are you staying?"

But the twins must not have heard him.

7

Warning Signs

"*B*ut what if some people weren't kind like the Willowbys?" asked Timothy, getting back to the subject of the hobo code when they were back home. "What if some people were mean? How would a hobo know that?"

"There were signs in the hobo code for that, too," said Grandpa. "For example, a dagger meant a dishonest man. Watch out. Not a good place to ask for work. Or there might be a picture of a comb."

"A *comb*?!" said Timothy, Titus, and Sarah-Jane all together.

"What did *that* mean?" asked Timothy. "Beware of neat hair?"

"No," said Grandpa, laughing. "But think about it. A comb has teeth. The sign warned the hobo to beware of something else with teeth."

"A dog!" cried Titus. "Beware of the dog. Right?"

"Right," said Grandpa.

"Woof!" said Gubbio happily. He knew a few key words—like dog—but he couldn't always follow a conversation.

"You're back," said Grandma, coming into the kitchen. "Those developers called again while you were out."

"Arrrghh!" said Grandpa and the cousins.

Grandma laughed. "They said they were afraid they hadn't been clear enough about their plans. They said they wanted to use the house and land for low-cost housing and that they'd like to talk to you about that."

"Really?" said Grandpa. "That's the first I've heard about that. Well, I guess I should at least hear what they have to say. Then I can see if it's in keeping with Mrs. Willowby's wishes. Would you call them back for me? Tell them I can meet them at the cottage later this afternoon."

"Will do," said Grandma.

Grandpa headed for his study, and the

cousins went along with him. He said he had an old book that might have some more of the hobo code in it.

Of all the places on earth, Grandpa's study was one of Titus's favorites. He loved the worn leather chairs. He loved the big, wooden desk. He loved the rows and rows and rows of books. Most of all he loved a little plaque on the wall, because it seemed exactly right for his grandfather. He wasn't sure what it all meant. But he had loved it ever since he had learned to read.

> *Life is short*
> *and we have never too much time*
> *for gladdening the hearts*
> *of those who are traveling*
> *the dark journey with us.*
> *Oh, be swift to love,*
> *make haste to be kind.*
>
> —*Henri Frederick Amiel*

Grandpa had once explained that "dark journey" was another way of saying "life." He said that sometimes life seems dark because we're sad and lonely. And sometimes life seems dark just because we never know what lies ahead. Grandpa had explained that life is like a journey for everyone and that we all need to be kind to one another because we are all fellow travelers.

Today the little plaque reminded Titus of the hoboes and how they left helpful signs for one another.

The cousins found a page of hobo signs in the book. Grandpa said they could borrow it to copy the signs into their code books.

Grandpa looked tired, Titus thought. He looked as if he had a lot on his mind, like keeping his promise to Mrs. Willowby.

Titus saw something in the book. He copied it onto a piece of scratch paper and held it out for his grandfather to see. It was a picture of two overlapping circles:

Grandpa studied the drawing for a moment, trying to recall what it meant. Suddenly he smiled.

The sign meant, "Don't give up."

8

Chalk Talk

*T*he cousins loved the junk drawer in their grandparents' kitchen. It was the best place in the world to hunt for little treasures.

When the cousins were little, they had never questioned how it was that exactly the right treat showed up at exactly the right time. And in the junk drawer, of all places.

But now they were older and wiser. And they were getting suspicious. Like today, when they found exactly what they needed there.

First they had finished copying the hobo signs into their code books. (The cats had left them alone, because Grandma was making a little quilt for a baby shower. And if there was one thing the cats loved more than climbing on

Titus, it was climbing on Grandma when she was sewing.)

And then the cousins had wanted to practice the code by drawing on the sidewalk. And what should they find in the junk drawer but washable chalk for drawing on the sidewalk.

"Hmmm," said Titus. "Very in-ter-es-ting."

"Downright weird, if you ask me," said Timothy.

"How does she *know*?" asked Sarah-Jane.

They decided there were some things not even detectives could find out. So they just left their own mysterious thank-you note. A chalk drawing on the front of the drawer. A picture of a smiling cat.

Then they took the chalk outside to practice. With practice, they got really good at using the code.

They learned how to tell one another the direction in which they were traveling:

gentleman	kind-hearted woman	safe camp, good jungle
go left	nothing	very good	go right
dishonest man	bad dog	don't give up
go straight ahead	bad water	all right, good place
keep quiet	these people will help you if you're sick	danger

They learned how to warn about bad water:

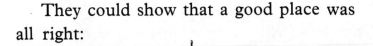

And how to show which people would help you if you were sick:

They could show that a good place was all right:

And they could tell you where you would get nothing:

They even knew how to say with pictures "Keep quiet":

And "Danger":

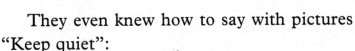

Granted, it was hard to say how any of this would come in handy. But one thing the cousins knew from experience: you never could tell.

9

No Twins

*I*t was something Titus had noticed—whenever you learned something new and exciting, you wanted to teach it to someone else.

Also, as much as he and his cousins liked playing together, they liked playing with other kids, too.

So it seemed as if all three of them got the same good idea at the same time: Show the hobo code to Matthew and Amanda!

This made sense, because Matthew and Amanda had been as fascinated as the cousins were with the little pictures Titus had found on the tree. They had hung on Grandpa's every word when he was telling about hoboes. And they had even named their cat Hobo.

There was just one problem with Matthew

and Amanda: Where were they?

"You know what's kind of funny?" Titus began.

"Funny ha-ha? Or funny weird?" asked Timothy.

"Funny weird."

"What is?"

"The way Matthew and Amanda just sort of took off like that," said Titus.

"Yes, now that you mention it," agreed Sarah-Jane. "I mean, I think they liked us and everything. But they didn't hang around long enough for us to invite them over."

"And they didn't invite us to their place, either," said Timothy.

"Maybe it's not their house," said Sarah-Jane. "They said they were just visiting. But still . . ."

Titus said, "Well, if they're visiting friends, I don't see how we can find out who they're staying with.

"But if they're staying at a bed and breakfast or a motel, we could maybe find them. We could call and see if any place has a family named Jennings with twins staying there."

Timothy and Sarah-Jane thought this was

as good an idea as any. So they asked their grandmother if they could use the phone. And they started calling. There were about a bazillion motels in the resort town.

At first it was fun. They took turns. They started with the places that were closest to the cottage and sort of worked their way out.

Then, after a while, the calling got pretty tedious. But the cousins knew that detective work could be that way sometimes. And it was worth it when you finally found what you were looking for.

Except sometimes you *didn't* find what you were looking for. They found a couple of families named Jennings all right.

But none with ten-year-old twins.

10

The Accident

*A*ll in all it had been a very frustrating experience. So the cousins felt the need to get out and move around. They were allowed to go off on their bikes by themselves as long as they wore their helmets, and stayed together, and got back by a certain time.

Without exactly planning to, they rode back over to the cottage. It looked so cozy and peaceful. What would happen to it, Titus wondered. Who would live there?

The cousins got off their bikes and walked around the cottage, peeking in the windows.

Then they found a way to get under the high front porch. As detectives, they were always looking for good hiding places. If you didn't mind a little dirt—which the cousins didn't—this was a wonderful hiding place.

It was especially good because you had to pull out a loose latticework board to get through. Then once you were in, you could pull the board back in place. You could easily see out through the holes. But it made it almost impossible for people on the other side to see the hiders.

"This is EXcellent!" said Titus.

"Neat-O!" agreed Timothy.

"So cool!" said Sarah-Jane.

But there wasn't a lot to do once they had found the place. And there wasn't actually anything to hide from. And after a while they needed sunlight and air.

So they crawled out and got back on their bikes. They rode off in the direction Matthew and Amanda had taken earlier, down a gravel road.

Everything was going fine until Timothy suddenly hit a bump. His bike skidded on the gravel, Timothy lost his balance, and before he could stop himself, he was thrown to the ground.

"Tim! Tim! Are you all right?" cried Sarah-Jane and Titus, rushing to his side.

Timothy sat up carefully. Nothing seemed to be broken.

"But what about your chin?" asked Titus. "You must have cut it on something. It's bleeding like crazy!"

Fortunately, Timothy had a clean handkerchief, and he held it to his chin. But the cousins knew they had to get help fast.

The problem was, they seemed to be out in the middle of nowhere. There were no houses or stores that they could see. And they desperately needed to get to a phone.

They were just trying to stay calm and *think* when suddenly something else happened.

Something leaped out of the bushes at the side of the road. It landed with a "thwup!" on Titus's shoulder.

11

Fast Help

*H*obo!

Titus knew a cat wasn't like a dog. You couldn't say, "Hobo, get help!" and expect anything to happen.

But he also realized that Hobo's being there might be a good sign. It might mean that help was nearby.

Titus jumped up and yelled, "Matthew! Amanda! Are you there? We need help!"

Sarah-Jane caught on right away. "Amanda!" she yelled. "Matthew! If you're there, come help us!"

Timothy caught on right away, too, but he couldn't yell because of his chin.

Almost immediately the cousins heard pounding footsteps. Matthew and Amanda appeared over a little ridge. With them was a lady who looked so much like them she had to be their mother.

Mrs. Jennings rushed to Timothy and took a look at the cut. She murmured something that sounded to Titus like "poor little guy." But it didn't sound babyish. It just sounded nice. It sounded like someone who was sorry for you but who knew everything was going to be all right.

The words from his grandfather's plaque popped into Titus's head—make haste to be kind. He also thought of the picture signs for a kindhearted woman and people who would help you if you were sick.

"I don't think it's too bad," Mrs. Jennings said. "But it will probably need stitches. We move our chins so much talking and eating that it's a hard place for a cut to heal. Let's get you to the campground. It's just over the ridge. We'll wash off the cut and I'll drive—Timothy, is it?—to the hospital. You can call your parents to meet us there."

"We're visiting our grandparents," explained Sarah-Jane. "Our grandfather is a pastor here. Pastor Gordon."

48

Mrs. Jennings nodded. "That's good. That means they probably know him at the hospital, right? You can use the phone at the campground office to call him."

Even with his cut chin, Timothy seemed to still have his mind on detective work. He mumbled to Titus and Sarah-Jane, "Why didn't we think of looking for Matthew and Amanda at the campground? The one place we didn't think to look is the place we found them."

All this time Matthew and Amanda had been looking worried about Timothy. But now they looked embarrassed—and kind of mad about looking embarrassed.

When Titus saw their station wagon, he realized why. The backseat was fixed up almost like an extra room.

Matthew and Amanda weren't camping for the fun of it. This was where they lived.

12

The Secret Hideout

"*I*t's not so bad," said Matthew with a careless little shrug. "Rainy days are the worst, of course. And we don't know what will happen after Labor Day."

"That's when the campground closes for the season," explained Amanda. "We'll have to move for sure. We just don't know where. Daddy is looking for a job all the time. He makes some money with odd jobs. But not enough to—"

"We get by," Matthew interrupted gruffly.

Amanda sighed wistfully. "I just love this little house."

The five of them were gathered again on the front porch of Mrs. Willowby's cottage. No one knew what to say to Amanda. Titus had the feeling that she came over here a lot to play and that Matthew just trailed along behind her. Matthew probably loved the house every bit as much as Amanda did. But Titus had the feeling that Matthew didn't see the point of hanging around something you wanted with all your heart if you could never have it.

At the hospital, Titus had managed to pull Grandpa aside and explain privately about where Matthew and Amanda lived. Titus knew he was explaining things especially well. And even though Grandpa hadn't said a lot, he had listened intently, as if he were thinking hard about something.

At the hospital, Grandma and Grandpa had thanked Mrs. Jennings over and over for her kindness to Timothy, who had gotten three stitches in his chin.

Grandma had wanted Timothy to go home and lie down. But she knew as well as Titus and Sarah-Jane did that getting Timothy to take a nap would be like getting him to eat pineapple or coconut. It just wasn't going to happen.

So the five kids had been allowed to ride over to the cottage on the condition that Timothy didn't "overdo it."

They had left their bikes in the trees behind the cottage. And now they were just hanging out on the porch in the shade of what they called "The Hobo Tree."

No one knew what to say when Amanda said she loved the house. To break the silence, Titus said, "We can show you something interesting we found. . . ."

He looked at Sarah-Jane and Timothy before he said any more. He didn't want to say anything about the secret hideout without their permission. They nodded, giving him the go-ahead. So Titus explained to the twins about the way to get under the porch.

"It's so cool," said Sarah-Jane. "We're always on the lookout for good hiding places because of being the T.C.D.C."

"What's a 'teesy-deesy'?" asked Amanda.

"It's letters," explained Timothy.

"Capital T. Capital C. Capital D. Capital C. It stands for the Three Cousins Detective Club."

Matthew and Amanda were clearly impressed with all this detective stuff. They had already learned some more of the hobo code from the cousins, and now they wanted to see the hideout.

There was plenty of room for all five kids. Make that five kids and a cat. Hobo had found them at the cottage, and now he insisted on exploring the hideout with them.

They had just gotten settled with the latticework in place when they heard something. A car pulled up in front, and three men got out. They came and stood just a few inches from where the cousins and the twins were hiding.

Titus couldn't help thinking it would look kind of stupid if they all crawled out now. Apparently the others were thinking the same thing, because nobody moved. They would just have to wait till the men went away.

Then one of the men said to the others, "OK. Let's get our story straight before the good pastor gets here. It's not going to be easy to put something over on Rev. Gordon."

Quickly Titus drew something in the dirt. There was just enough light for the others to see. They took one look and nodded silently.

For Titus had drawn:

And:

Keep Quiet.
Danger.

13

The Sign of the Dagger

"OK, here's the deal," said the first man. "We know that Old Lady Willowby left some kind of wacky instructions in her will. And Rev. Gordon feels 'duty-bound to honor her wishes,' as he puts it. Give me a break. He won't even say what the old lady wanted."

Titus bit down hard on his lip. It was hard not to go charging out and say, "For your information, Buster, Mrs. Willowby was *not* 'wacky.' She was one of the kindest people I ever met. And furthermore—my grandfather keeps his promises. What else would you expect? And furthermore—my grandfather does *not* go blabbing stuff that people tell him in private. Not to you or anybody else. It's called honor. Look it up."

Titus doubted he could really have gotten all that out.

Besides, something told him it was wiser to keep quiet. He felt the tiniest ripple of angry movement on either side of him. And he guessed that Timothy and Sarah-Jane were itching to do the same thing he wanted to.

But they kept still. They had trained themselves to do that. Matthew and Amanda copied them and kept quiet, too. Even Hobo was still. He was curled up sound asleep under Titus's chin.

"So where does that leave us?" asked the second man. "We don't know what the old lady wanted. So how can we offer something Rev. Gordon will take?"

"We can't tell him what we're really planning," said the third man. "To tear down the cottage and build another luxury motel on the land."

Under the porch, Amanda clapped her hand over her mouth. Other than that, no one moved.

"No, of course we can't tell him that," said the first man impatiently. "That's why we're going to talk to Rev. Gordon about the need for low-income housing. Lead him to believe we're going to put up a small apartment building for the poor or something like that."

"Right," said the second man. "If he thinks it's going for such a good cause, he'll probably be willing to sell us the place—no matter what the will says."

"How can he say no?" asked the third man. "And by the time he finds out what we're really building, it will be too late."

"Just follow my lead and everything will be all right," said the first man. "We have to be careful not to lay it on too thick. We don't want him to get suspicious."

The men walked off toward the road to wait for Pastor Gordon.

But no way was Pastor Gordon going to fall for their scam.

That was because just as he rode up, Titus crept out from under the porch. He took a piece of washable chalk from his pocket and drew a big picture on the door of the house:

A dagger. A hobo warning.
Beware of dishonest men.

14

A Problem Solved

*T*he men turned to see what Grandpa was looking at.

Titus thought—with a certain amount of satisfaction—that they looked alarmed to see him there. He could almost hear them wondering: Where did that kid come from? Did he overhear what we said? Does Rev. Gordon know him? Why is he drawing on the door?

If the men were surprised to see Titus, they were flabbergasted to see four other kids crawl out from under the porch. Make that four kids and a crabby cat. Hobo didn't take kindly to being wakened from a nap—no matter what the reason.

Grandpa hurried over. "What's all this about?" he asked.

It took a while—quite a while—to explain what they were doing under the porch and what they had overheard when they were under there.

Grandpa turned to confront the men, who had been planning to lie to him. But their car was already skidding out of the driveway.

"Well, Grandpa," said Timothy. "I don't think you'll be getting any more calls from them."

"That's right," agreed Sarah-Jane. "But it still doesn't solve Grandpa's problem of what to do with Mrs. Willowby's house."

"On the contrary," said Grandpa. "I have just about solved that problem. Thanks to you three."

"Us!" said Titus. "What did *we* do?"

"We'll talk about it at dinner," said Grandpa.

And the cousins knew from experience they wouldn't get another word out of him till then.

"By the way," said Grandpa, turning to Matthew and Amanda. "Tell your parents that Mrs. Gordon and I would like to invite them to dinner tonight. There's something I need to talk to them about. You come, too, of course. You can even bring Hobo." He paused and added with a straight face, "It's like Titus always says. You can never have too many cats."

15

Home

Gubbio usually loved it when company came to dinner. But when he saw that these people had brought a cat with them, he looked at Titus as if to say, "How could you do this to me?"

So when Titus showed Mr. and Mrs. Jennings into Grandpa's study before supper, Gubbio went along. In the study he could be safely away from all those annoying cats.

That meant that Gubbio heard all that Grandpa and Mr. and Mrs. Jennings talked about. But no one else did.

All that the cousins and the twins knew was that something wonderful must have happened—even though both Mr. and Mrs. Jennings looked as if they had been crying.

"What's going on?" asked Amanda a little anxiously as they sat down to dinner.

"Oh, not much," said her father. "We just bought a house. That's all."

"A house!" cried Matthew. "What house? Where did we get the money to buy a house?"

Grandpa smiled. "It's like this. Mrs. Willowby made me promise I would find the right people and sell them her cottage."

Amanda gasped.

Everyone laughed. Grandpa went on. "Mrs. Willowby wanted her cottage to go to people who really needed it. She wanted people who would love it and take care of it. And she wanted people who would in turn be kind to others. Well, I found just such people in the Jennings family. Or rather—my grandchildren found them. And Mrs. Willowby said when I found these people I was to sell them her cottage for the grand sum of one dollar."

"A *dollar*?" cried Matthew. "Mrs. Willowby sold us her house for a *dollar*?!"

"That's just the kind of person she was," said Grandma with a gentle, remembering smile.

"Oh!" cried Amanda and Sarah-Jane to-

gether. "It's just the *sweetest house!*"

And, though he might not have put it that way, Titus had to agree.

He wished everyone in the whole world who needed a house could have one just like it.

But Mrs. Willowby had done what she could. And that's all anyone could do, Titus thought. It was what the plaque in his grandfather's study meant when it said:

> *Life is short*
> *and we have never too much time*
> *for gladdening the hearts*
> *of those who are traveling*
> *the dark journey with us.*
> *Oh, be swift to love,*
> *make haste to be kind.*

The End